Avalanches

by Lisa Bullard

Lerner Publications Company • Minneapolis

For my brother Joel, with love

Photo Acknowledgments

The images in this book are used with the permission of: © Photodisc/Getty Images, all backgrounds; © Fabrice Coffrini/Getty Images, p. 4; © Medford Taylor/National Geographic/Getty Images, p. 6; © StockShot/Alamy, pp. 7, 12, 20; © Scott Warren/Aurora/Getty Images, p. 8; © Whit Richardson/Aurora/Getty Images, p. 10; © Tim Laman/ National Geographic/Getty Images, p. 11; © Papilio/Alamy, p. 13; © Marc Muench/Stone/Getty Images, p. 14; © Kevin Schafer/Alamy, p. 15; © James Balog/Stone/Getty Images, p. 16; © Michael S. Quinton/National Geographic/ Getty Images, p. 18; © Extreme Sports Photo/Alamy, p. 19; AP Photo/The News Tribune, Peter Haley, p. 21; AP Photo/Douglas C. Pizac, p. 22; © Steimer, C./Peter Arnold, Inc., p. 23; © Vegar Abelsnes Photography/ Stone/Getty Images, p. 24; © Norbert Falco/Maxppp/ZUMA Press, p. 26; © © Brett Pelletier/Dreamstime.com, p. 27; Illustration on p. 28 by © Bill Hauser/Independent Picture Service.

Front cover: © StockShot/Alamy.
Back cover: © Photodisc/Getty Images.

Text copyright © 2009 by Lerner Publishing Group, Inc.

Lerner Publications Company
A division of Lerner Publishing Group, Inc.
241 First Avenue North
Minneapolis, MN 55401

Website address: www.lernerbooks.com

Words in **bold type** are explained in a glossary on page 31.

Library of Congress Cataloging-in-Publication Data

Bullard, Lisa.
    Avalanches / by Lisa Bullard.
        p.   cm. — (Pull ahead books. Forces of nature)
    Includes index.
    ISBN 978–0–8225–8827–6 (lib. bdg. : alk. paper)
    1. Avalanches—Juvenile literature. I. Title
QC929.A8B85 2009
551.57'848–dc22   2007038933

Manufactured in the United States of America
1 2 3 4 5 6 – BP – 14 13 12 11 10 09

Table of Contents

What Is an Avalanche?

Suddenly, a huge amount of snow roars down the mountain. Everything in its path is dragged with it. This powerful downhill slide is called an **avalanche**.

An avalanche can also be sliding rocks or mud. But the word *avalanche* usually means "a snowslide."

Avalanches happen where the land is steep. They slide down **slopes** such as mountains.

This person looks closely at snow layers. He is checking to see whether an avalanche might happen.

How Avalanches Happen

Mountains are some of the snowiest places on Earth. Each snowstorm makes a new layer of snow. Each layer rests on top of the one that fell before. Sometimes the layers do not stick together. A weak layer forms.

Sometimes the top layer doesn't stick.
A little snow slips off the snow pile.

It slides downhill. It pulls more snow with it. This is called a **loose-snow avalanche**.

Sometimes a big block of snow breaks off all at once. It slides off a weak layer buried under the top layers.

This is called a **slab avalanche**. The slab roars downhill with huge force.

Many things can cause avalanches. Some are set off by wind. Some start from the weight of falling snow.

This avalanche fell on Mount Rainier in the state of Washington.

Scientists believe there are more than a million avalanches each year. Most happen far away from people.

An avalanche in Alta, Utah, buried these cars.

Dangers of Avalanches

Avalanches are a danger to some mountain towns. People build snow fences to protect their town. But this is not always enough. Large avalanches can bury buildings. They overturn train cars. They can knock down trees.

People travel into high mountains.
Some people go to mountain climb.
Others ski or snowboard. Some
people ride **snowmobiles**.

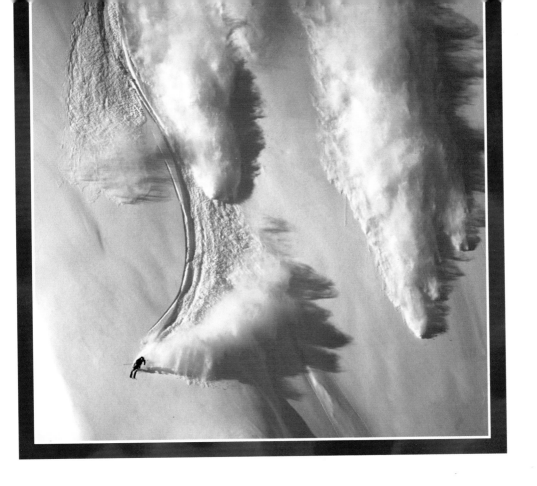

People can start avalanches. Just one person can set off a giant snowslide.

Avalanches hurt and kill some winter
sports fans every year. Some people
break bones as they tumble downhill.

Others are buried deep in snow. The snow gets packed hard around them.

Rescuers use a helicopter to look for missing skiers after an avalanche.

Rescuers try to help. They use long **probes** to find the buried person.

A rescue dog sniffs out a person buried in an avalanche.

Rescue dogs can find people much faster. But trained dogs are not always nearby.

Hikers check a map to stay safe in avalanche areas.

Staying Safe

People sometimes enjoy winter sports in places that have avalanches. They need to plan ahead. They should bring along avalanche shovels and rescue tools. They should never travel alone.

They should also wear a radio **beacon**. It is used to track someone buried in snow.

A radio beacon can lead rescuers to someone buried under the snow.

Winter sports can be fun. But learn about avalanche safety before you hit the slopes!

THE PATH OF AN AVALANCHE

There are three parts to an avalanche path. The avalanche begins in the starting zone. Then it follows a track downhill. Finally, there is the runout zone. This is where the avalanche comes to a stop. Sometimes new avalanches will follow the path of an old avalanche. So it is important to stay safe in those areas.

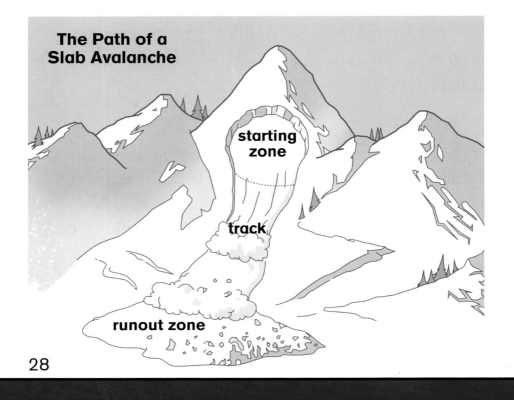

The Path of a Slab Avalanche

starting zone

track

runout zone

Avalanche Facts

- You cannot usually outrun an avalanche. Some avalanches can travel faster than a race car!

- Some ski resorts have learned how to prevent big avalanches. They start small avalanches using explosives. This clears away dangerous piles of snow.

- Long ago, people thought avalanches were caused by evil spirits or dragons hiding in the mountains.

- Most people think a loud noise can start an avalanche. This is not usually true.

- Most avalanches happen during or just after a storm.

- One giant avalanche happened on Mount Sanford, Alaska, in 1981. The avalanche traveled almost 8 miles (13 kilometers) before stopping. It even went over the top of a 3,000-foot-high (900 meters) mountain in its way!

- Some scientists study the snow to try to tell when and where an avalanche might happen.

Further Reading

Books

Drohan, Michelle Ingber. *Avalanches*. New York: Rosen Publishing Group, 1999.

Hopping, Lorraine Jean. *Avalanche!* New York: Scholastic, 2000.

Silverman, Maida. *Snow Search Dogs*. New York: Bearport Publishing Company, 2005.

Websites

Avalanches
http://www.nationalgeographic.com/ngkids/0301/
This National Geographic Kids site offers avalanche facts and safety tips. You can also watch an avalanche video.

Snowflakes and Avalanches
http://www.sciencenewsforkids.org/articles/20060118/Feature1.asp
This Science News for Kids site gives many details about the science behind avalanches.

Winter Storms
http://www.weatherwizkids.com/winter_storms.htm
This Weather Wiz Kids site offers lots of information about snow and winter storms. It also has avalanche safety tips.

Glossary

avalanche: a large amount of snow that slides down a mountain

beacon: a kind of radio that you wear under your clothes and use to be safe in an avalanche. It gives off a signal that other beacons can pick up. This shows rescuers where you are if you are buried in snow.

loose-snow avalanche: an avalanche caused when a little snow slips off a pile and picks up more snow as it slides downhill

probes: long, thin rods used to poke into the snow to look for buried persons

slab avalanche: an avalanche caused when a block of snow breaks off a snow pile

slopes: ground that slants up and down, like the side of a mountain

snowmobiles: machines that people ride over snow

Index